Contents

THE SECRET SEVEN

ENID BLYTON

a division of Hodder Headline Limited

First published in Great Britain in 1949
by Hodder and Stoughton
This edition 2002

For further information on Enid Blyton please contact
www.blyton.com

10 9 8 7 6 5 4

A Catalogue record for this book is available from the British Library

ISBN 0 340 79636 7

Typeset by Hewer Text Ltd, Edinburgh
Printed and bound in Great Britain
by Clays Ltd, St Ives plc

The paper and board used in this paperback by Hodder Children's Books are natural recyclable products made from wood grown in sustainable forests. The manufacturing processes conform to the environmental regulations of the country of origin.

Hodder Children's Books
a division of Hodder Headline Limited
338 Euston Road
London NW1 3BH

[1]

Plans for an S.S. meeting

'We'd better have a meeting of the Secret Seven,' said Peter to Janet. 'We haven't had one for ages.'

'Oh, yes, let's!' said Janet, shutting her book with a bang. 'It isn't that we've forgotten about the Society, Peter – it's just that we've had such a lot of exciting things to do in the Christmas holidays we simply haven't had time to call a meeting.'

'But we must,' said Peter. 'It's no good having a Secret Society unless we use it. We'd better send out messages to the others.'

'Five notes to write,' groaned Janet. 'You're quicker at writing than I am, Peter – you write three and I'll write two.'

'Woof!' said Scamper, the golden spaniel.

'Yes, I know you'd love to write one, too, if you could,' said Janet, patting the silky golden head. 'You can carry one in your mouth to deliver. That can be *your* job, Scamper.'

'What shall we say?' said Peter, pulling a piece of paper towards him and chewing the end of his pen as he tried to think of the words.

'Well – we'd better tell them to come here, I think,' said Janet. 'We could use the old shed at the bottom of the garden for a meeting-place, couldn't we? Mummy lets us play there in the winter because it's next to the boiler that heats the greenhouse, and it's quite warm.'

'Right,' said Peter, and he began to write. 'I'll do this message first, Janet, and you can copy it. Let's see – we want one for Pam, one for Colin, one for Jack, one for Barbara – who's the seventh of us? I've forgotten.'

'George, of course,' said Janet. 'Pam, Colin, Jack, Barbara, George, you and me – that's the seven – the Secret Seven. It sounds nice, doesn't it?'

The Seven Society was one that Peter and Janet had invented. They thought it was great fun to have a band of boys and girls who knew the password, and who wore the badge – a button with S.S. on.

'There you are,' said Peter, passing his sheet of paper to Janet. 'You can copy that.'

'It doesn't need to be my *best* writing, does it?' said Janet. 'I'm so slow if I have to do my best writing.'

'Well – so long as it's readable,' said Peter. 'It hasn't got to go by post.'

Janet read what Peter had written: 'IMPORTANT. A meeting of the Secret Seven will be held tomorrow morning in the shed at the bottom of our garden at 10 o'clock. Please give PASSWORD.'

'Oh – what *was* the last password we

had?' said Janet in alarm. 'It's so long since we had a meeting that I've forgotten.'

'Well, it's a good thing for you that you've got me to remind you,' said Peter. 'Our latest password was Wenceslas, because we wanted a Christmassy one. Fancy you forgetting that!'

'Oh, yes, of course. Good King Wenceslas,' said Janet. 'Oh, dear – now I've gone and made a mistake in this note already. I really mustn't talk while I'm doing it.'

There was a silence as the two of them wrote their notes. Janet always wrote with her tongue out, which made her look very funny. But she said she couldn't write properly unless her tongue *was* out, so out it had to come.

Peter finished first. He let Scamper lick the envelopes. He was good at that; he had such a nice big wet tongue.

'You're a very licky dog,' said Peter, 'so you must be pleased when you have things like this to lick. It's a pity we're not putting stamps on the letters, then you could lick those, too.'

'Now shall we go and deliver the secret messages?' said Janet. 'Mummy said we could go out; it's a nice sunny morning – even if it is cold!'

'Woof! woof!' said Scamper, running to the door when he heard the word 'out'. He pawed at the door impatiently.

Soon the three of them were out in the frost and snow. It was lovely. They went to Colin's first. He was out, so they left the note with his mother.

Then to George's. He was in, and was very excited when he heard about the meeting to be held in the shed.

Then to Pam's. Jack was there too, so Peter left two notes. Then there was only Barbara left. She was away!

'Bother!' said Peter. But when he heard she was coming back that night he was pleased. 'Will she be able to come and see us tomorrow morning?' he asked Barbara's mother, and she said yes, she thought so.

'Well, that's all five,' said Janet as they turned to go home. 'Come on, Scamper. We'll go for a run in the park.'

They had a lovely time in the park, throwing snowballs and making tracks in the crisp new snow. Scamper discovered a frozen pond. He stepped on to the ice but his legs slid out from under him. He struggled to stand up, but couldn't. In the end the laughing children had to haul him off the pond.

Scamper was cross. He turned and growled at the pond. He didn't understand it at all. He could drink it in the summer, and paddle in it – now look at it! Something strange had happened, and he didn't like it.

That afternoon the two children and Scamper went down to the old shed. It was warm, because the boiler was going well nearby to heat the big greenhouse. Peter looked round.

'It feels quite cosy. Let's arrange boxes for seats – and get the old garden cushions out. And we'll ask Mummy if we can have some lemonade or something, and biscuits. We'll have a really proper meeting!'

They pulled out some boxes and fetched the old cushions. They laid sacks on the ground for a carpet, and Janet cleaned a little shelf to put the lemonade and biscuits on, if their mother let them have some.

'There are only five boxes that are sittable on,' said Peter. 'Someone will have to sit on the floor.'

'Oh, no – there are two enormous flowerpots in the corner over there,' said Janet. 'Let's drag them out and turn them upside down. They'll be fine to sit on then.'

So, with the five boxes and the two flowerpots, there were seats for everyone.

The bell rang for tea. 'Well, we've just

finished nicely,' said Peter. 'I know what I'm going to do tonight, Janet.'

'What?' asked Janet.

'I'm going to draw two big letter Ss,' said Peter, 'and colour them green – cut them out, mount them on cardboard, and then stick them to the door of the shed.'

'Oh, yes – S.S. – Secret Seven,' said Janet. 'That would be *grand*!'

[2]

The Secret Seven Society

The next morning five children made their way to Old Mill House, where Peter and Janet lived. It took its name from the ruined mill that stood up on the hill, some distance away, which had not been used for many years.

George came first. He walked down the garden and came to the shed. The first thing he saw was the sign on the door, S.S. There it was, bold and clear in bright green.

He knocked on the door. There was a silence. He knocked again. Still no reply, though he felt sure that Peter and Janet were there because he was certain he had seen Janet's face at the little window of the shed.

He heard a snuffling under the door.

That must be Scamper! He knocked again, impatiently.

'Give the password, silly!' said Peter's voice.

'Oh, I forgot,' said George. 'Wenceslas!'

The door opened at once. George grinned and went in. He looked round. 'This is very cosy. Is it to be our meeting-place these hols?'

'Yes. It's nice and warm here,' said Peter. 'Where's your badge? Your button with S.S. on?'

'Bother – I forgot it,' said George. 'I hope I haven't lost it.'

'You're not a very good member,' said Janet sternly. 'Forgetting to say the password, and forgetting your badge as well.'

'Sorry,' said George. 'To tell you the truth I'd almost forgotten about the Secret Society too!'

'Well, you don't deserve to belong then,' said Peter.

'Just because we haven't met for some time! I do think—'

There was another knock at the door. It was Pam and Barbara. There was silence in the shed. Everyone was listening for the password.

'Wenceslas,' hissed Barbara, in such a peculiar voice that everyone jumped.

'Wenceslas,' whispered Pam. The door opened, and in they went.

'Good – you're both wearing your badges,' said Peter, pleased. 'Now where are Colin and Jack? They're late.'

Jack was waiting for Colin at the gate. He had forgotten the password! Oh dear, whatever could it be? He thought of all sorts of things – Nowell – Wise Men – what *could* it be? He felt sure it was something to do with Christmas carols.

He didn't like to go to the meeting-place without knowing the password. Peter could be very strict. Jack didn't like being ticked off in front of people, and he racked his brains to try to think of the word. He saw Colin away in the distance and decided to wait for him. Colin would be sure to know the word!

'Hallo!' said Colin, as he came up. 'Seen the others yet?'

'I saw Pam and Barbara going in,' said Jack. 'Do you know the password, Colin?'

'Of course I do,' said Colin.

'I bet you don't!' said Jack.

'Well, I do – it's Wenceslas!' said Colin. 'Aha – sucks to you, Jack – you thought I didn't know it!'

'Thanks for telling me,' grinned Jack. 'I'd forgotten it. Don't tell Peter. Come on down the path. Hey! Look at the S.S. for Secret Seven on the door.'

They knocked. 'WENCESLAS,' said Colin in a very loud voice.

The door opened quickly and Peter's angry face looked out. 'Whatever are you shouting for? Do you want everyone in the village to know our password, you fool?'

'Sorry,' said Colin, going in. 'Anyway, there's nobody but us to hear.'

'Wenceslas,' said Jack, seeing that Peter was not going to let him in without the password. The door shut and the Seven settled down. Peter and Janet took the flowerpots for themselves. Everyone else sat on the boxes.

'This is a great meeting-place,' said George. 'Warm and cosy, and right away from the house.'

'Yes. I must say you and Janet have made it very comfortable,' said Barbara. 'Even a little curtain at the window.'

Peter looked round at the little company. 'We'll have our meeting first, and then we'll have the eats and drinks,' he said.

Everyone's eyes went to the neat little shelf behind Colin. On it were arranged seven mugs, a plate of oatmeal biscuits, and a bottle of some dark-looking liquid. Whatever could it be?

'First of all,' went on Peter, 'we must arrange a new password, because Wenceslas doesn't seem right for after Christmas – besides, Colin yelled it out at the top of his voice, so everyone probably knows it now.'

'Don't be so—' began Colin, but Peter frowned at him sternly.

'Don't interrupt. I'm the head of this society, and I say we will choose a new password. Also I see that two of you are not wearing your badges. George and Colin.'

'I told you I forgot about mine,' said George. 'I'll find it when I get home.'

'And I think I must have *lost* mine,' said Colin. 'I didn't forget it. I hunted all over the place. My mother says she'll make me another tonight.'

'Right,' said Peter. 'Now what about a new password?'

'Hey-diddle-diddle,' said Pam, with a giggle.

'Be sensible,' said Peter. 'This society is a serious one, not a silly one.'

'I thought of one last night,' said Jack. 'Would "Weekdays" do?'

'What's the sense of that?' asked Peter.

'Well – there are seven days in a week, aren't there – and we're the Seven Society,' said Jack. 'I thought it was rather good.'

'Oh, I see. Yes – it *is* rather good,' said Peter. 'Though actually, there are only five *week*days! Hands up those who think it's good.'

Everybody's hand went up. Yes, 'Weekdays' was a good idea for a password for the Seven! Jack looked pleased.

'Actually I forgot our password today,' he confessed. 'I got it out of Colin. So I'm glad I've thought of a new one for us.'

'Well, nobody must forget this one,' said

Peter. 'It might be very important. Now what about some grub?'

'Delumptious,' said Barbara, and everyone laughed.

'Do you mean "delicious" or "scrumptious"?' asked Janet.

'Both, of course,' said Barbara. 'What's that peculiar-looking stuff in the bottle, Janet?'

Janet was shaking it vigorously. It was a dark purple and had little black things bobbing about in it.

'Mummy hadn't any lemonade to give us, and we didn't particularly want milk because we'd had lots for breakfast,' she said. 'So we suddenly thought of a pot of blackcurrant jam we had! This is blackcurrant tea!'

'We mixed it with boiling water and put some more sugar into it,' explained Peter. 'It's really good – in fact, it's scrumplicious!'

'Oh – *that's* a mixture of scrumptious and

delicious, too!' said Barbara with a squeal of laughter. 'Delumptious and scrumplicious – that just describes everything nicely.'

The blackcurrant tea really was good, and went very well with the oatmeal biscuits. 'It's good for colds, too,' said Janet, crunching up the skinny blackcurrants from her mug. 'So if anyone's getting a cold they probably won't.'

Everyone understood this peculiar statement and nodded. They set down their mugs and smacked their lips.

'It's a pity there's no more,' said Janet. 'But there wasn't an awful lot of jam left in the pot, or else we could have made heaps to drink.'

'Now, we have a little more business to discuss,' said Peter, giving Scamper a few crumbs to lick. 'It's no good having a Society unless we have some plan to follow – something to *do*.'

'Like we did in the summer,' said Pam.

know – when we collected money to se. d some disabled children to the seaside.'

'Yes. Well, has anyone any ideas?' said Peter.

Nobody had. 'It's not really a good time to try and help people after Christmas,' said Pam. 'I mean – everyone's had presents and been looked after, even the very poorest, oldest people in the village.'

'Can't we solve a mystery, or something like that?' suggested George. 'If we can't find something wrong to put right, we might be able to find a mystery to clear up.'

'What kind of a mystery do you mean?' asked Barbara, puzzled.

'I don't really know,' said George. 'We'd have to be on the lookout for one – you know, watch for something strange or peculiar – and solve it.'

'It sounds exciting,' said Colin. 'But I don't believe we'd find anything like that

– and if we did the police would have found it first!'

'Oh, well,' said Peter, 'we'll just have to keep our eyes open and wait and see. If anyone hears of any good deed we can do, or of any mystery that wants solving, they must at once call a meeting of the Secret Seven. Is that understood?'

Everyone said yes. 'And if we have anything to report we can come here to this Secret Seven shed and leave a note, can't we?' said George.

'That would be the best thing to do,' agreed Peter. 'Janet and I will be here each morning, and we'll look and see if any of you have left a note. I hope somebody does!'

'So do I. It's not much fun having a Secret Society that doesn't *do* anything,' said Colin. 'I'll keep a really good lookout. You never know when something might turn up.'

'Let's go and build snowmen in the field opposite the old house down by the stream,' said George, getting up. 'The snow's thick there. It would be fun. We could build quite an army of snowmen. They'd look funny standing in the field by themselves.'

'Oh, yes. Let's do that,' said Janet, who was tired of sitting still. 'I'll take this old shabby cap to put on one of the snowmen! It's been hanging in this shed for ages.'

'And I'll take this coat!' said Peter, dragging down a dirty, ragged coat from a nail. 'Goodness knows who it ever belonged to!'

And off they all went to the field by the stream to build an army of snowmen!

[3]

The cross old man

They didn't build an army, of course! They only had time to build four snowmen. The snow was thick and soft in the field, and it was easy to roll it into big balls and use them for the snowmen. Scamper had a lovely time helping them all.

Janet put the cap on one of the snowmen, and Peter put the old coat round his snowy shoulders. They found stones for his eyes and nose, and a piece of wood for his mouth. They gave him a stick under his arm. He looked the best of the lot.

'I suppose it's time to go home now,' said Colin at last. 'My dinner's at half-past twelve, worse luck.'

'We'd better all go home,' said Pam.

'We'll all have to wash and change our things and put our gloves to dry. Mine are soaking and oooh, my hands are cold!'

'So are mine. I know they'll hurt awfully as soon as they begin to get a bit warm,' said Barbara, shaking her wet hands up and down. 'They're beginning to now.'

They left the snowmen in the field and went out of the nearby gate. Opposite was an old house. It was empty except for one room at the bottom, where dirty curtains hung across the window.

'Who lives there?' asked Pam.

'Only a caretaker,' said Janet. 'He's very old and very deaf – and awfully bad-tempered.'

They hung over the gate and looked at the desolate old house.

'It's quite big,' said Colin. 'I wonder who it belongs to, and why they don't live in it.'

'Isn't the path up to the house lovely and smooth with snow?' said Janet. 'Not even the caretaker has trodden on it. I suppose he uses the back gate. Oh, Scamper – you naughty dog, come back!'

Scamper had squeezed under the gate and gone bounding up the smooth, snowy path. The marks of his feet were clearly to be seen. He barked joyfully.

The curtains at the ground-floor window moved and a cross, wrinkled old face looked out. Then the window was thrown up.

'You get out of here! Take your dog away! I won't have children or dogs here, pestering little varmints!'

Scamper stood and barked boldly at the old caretaker. He disappeared. Then a door opened at the side of the house and the old man appeared, with a big stick. He shook it at the alarmed children.

'I'll whack your dog till he's black and blue!' shouted the man.

'Scamper, Scamper, come here!' shouted

Peter. But Scamper seemed to have gone completely deaf. The caretaker advanced on him grimly, holding the stick up to hit the spaniel.

Peter pushed open the gate and tore up the path to Scamper, afraid he would be hurt.

'I'll take him, I'll take him!' he shouted to the old man.

'What's that you say?' said the cross old fellow, lowering his stick. 'What do you want to go and send your dog in here for?'

'I didn't. He came in himself!' called Peter, slipping his fingers into Scamper's collar.

'Speak up, I can't hear you,' bellowed the old man, as if it was Peter who was deaf and not himself. Peter bellowed back:

'I DIDN'T SEND MY DOG IN!'

'All right, all right, don't shout,' grumbled the caretaker. 'Don't you come back here again, that's all, or I'll send the police after you.'

He disappeared into the side door again. Peter marched Scamper down the drive and out of the gate.

'What a bad-tempered man,' he said to the others. 'He might have hurt Scamper awfully if he'd hit him with that great stick.'

Janet shut the gate. 'Now you and Scamper have spoilt the lovely smooth path,' she said. 'Goodness, there's the church clock striking a quarter to one. We'll really have to hurry!'

'We'll let you all know when the next meeting is!' shouted Peter, as they parted at the corner. 'And don't forget the password and your badges.'

They all went home. Jack was the first in because he lived very close. He rushed into the bathroom to wash his hands. Then he went to brush his hair.

'I'd better put my badge away,' he thought, and put up his hand to feel for it. But it wasn't there. He frowned and went into the bathroom. He must have dropped it.

He couldn't find it anywhere. He must have dropped it in the field when he was making the snowmen with the others. Bother! Blow!

'Mother's away, so she can't make me a new one,' he thought. 'And I'm sure Miss Ely wouldn't.'

Miss Ely was his sister's nanny. She liked Susie, Jack's sister, but she thought Jack was dirty, noisy and bad-mannered. He wasn't really, but somehow he never did behave very well with Miss Ely.

'I'll ask her if she *will* make one,' he decided. 'After all, I've been very good the last two days.'

Miss Ely might perhaps have said she would make him his badge if things hadn't suddenly gone wrong at dinner-time.

'*I* know where you've been this morning,' said Susie, slyly, when the three of them were at the table. 'Ha, ha. You've been to your silly Secret Society. You think I don't know anything about it. Well, I do!'

Jack glared at her. 'Shut up! You ought to know better than to talk about other people's secrets in public. You just hold that horrid, interfering tongue of yours.'

'Don't talk like that, Jack,' said Miss Ely at once.

'What's the password?' went on the annoying Susie. 'I know what the last one was because you wrote it down in your notebook so as not to forget and I saw it! It was—'

Jack kicked out hard under the table, meaning to get Susie on the shin. But most unfortunately Miss Ely's long legs were in the way. Jack's boot hit her hard on the ankle.

She gave a loud cry of pain. 'Oh! My ankle! How dare you, Jack! Leave the table and go without your dinner. I shall not speak another word to you all day long, if that is how you behave.'

'I'm awfully sorry, Miss Ely,' muttered Jack, scarlet with shame. 'I didn't mean to kick *you*.'

'It's the kicking that matters, not the person,' said Miss Ely, coldly. 'It doesn't make it any better knowing that you meant to kick Susie, not me. Leave the room, please.'

Jack went out. He didn't dare to slam the door, though he felt like it. He wasn't cross with Susie any more. He had caught sight of her face as he went out of the room, and had seen that she was alarmed and upset. She had meant to tease him, but she hadn't meant him to lose his dinner.

He kicked his toes against each step as he went upstairs. It was a pity he'd been sent out before the jam tarts were served. He liked those so much. Blow Miss Ely! Now she certainly wouldn't make a new badge for him, and probably he would be turned out of the Society for losing it. Peter had threatened to do that to anyone who turned up more than once without a badge.

I seem to remember something falling off me when I was making that last snowman, thought Jack. I think I'll go out and look this afternoon. I'd better go before it snows again, or I'll never find it.

But Miss Ely caught him as he was going out and stopped him. 'No, Jack. You are to stay in today, after that extraordinary behaviour of yours at the dinner-table,' she said sternly. 'You will not go out to play any more today.'

'But I want to go and find something I lost, Miss Ely,' argued Jack, trying to edge out.

'Did you hear what I said?' said Miss Ely, raising her voice, and poor Jack slid indoors again.

All right! He would simply go out that night then, and look with his torch. Miss Ely would *not* stop him from doing what he wanted to do!

[4]

What happened to Jack

Jack was as good as his word. He went up to bed at his usual time, after saying a polite good night to Miss Ely, but he didn't get undressed. He put on his coat and cap instead! He wondered whether he dared go downstairs and out of the garden door yet.

Perhaps I'd better wait and see if Miss Ely goes to bed early, he thought. She sometimes goes up to read in bed. I don't want to be caught. She'd only go and tell tales when Mother comes home.

So he took a book and sat down. Miss Ely waited for the nine o'clock news on the radio and then she locked up the house and came upstairs. Jack heard her shut the door of her room.

Good! Now he could go. He slipped his torch into his pocket, because it really was a very dark night. The moon was not yet up.

He crept downstairs quietly and went to the garden door. He undid it gently. The bolt gave a little squeak but that was all. He stepped into the garden. His feet sank quietly into the snow.

He made his way to the lane and went down it to the field, flashing his little torch as he went. The snow glimmered up, and there was a dim whitish light all round from it. He soon came to the field where they had built the snowmen, and he climbed over the gate.

The snowmen stood silently in a group together, almost as if they were watching and waiting for him. Jack didn't altogether like it. He thought one moved, and he drew his breath in sharply. But, of course, it hadn't. It was just his imagination.

'Don't be silly,' he told himself, sternly. 'You know they're only made of snow! Be sensible and look for your dropped button!'

He switched on his torch and the snowmen gleamed whiter than ever. The one with eyes and nose and mouth, with the cap and the coat on, seemed to look at him gravely as he hunted here and there. Jack turned his back on him.

'You may only have stone eyes, but you seem to be able to *look* with them, all the same,' he said to the silent snowman. 'Now don't go tapping me on the shoulder and make me jump!'

Then he suddenly gave an exclamation. He had found his badge! There lay the button in the snow, with S.S. embroidered on it, for Secret Seven. Hurrah! He must have dropped it here after all then.

He picked it up. It was wet with snow. He pinned it carefully on his coat. That really *was* a bit of luck to find it so easily. Now he could go home and get into bed. He was cold and sleepy.

His torch suddenly flickered, and then went out. 'Bother!' said Jack. 'The battery's gone. It *could* have lasted till I got home, really it could! Well, it's a good thing I know my way.'

He suddenly heard a noise down the lane, and saw the headlights of a car. It was coming very slowly. Jack was surprised. The lane led nowhere at all. Was the car lost? He'd better go and put the driver on the right road, if so. People often got lost when the roads were snowbound.

He went to the gate. The car came slowly by and then Jack saw that it was towing something – something rather big. What could it possibly be?

The boy strained his eyes to see. It wasn't big enough for a removal van, and yet it looked rather like the shape of one. It wasn't a caravan either, because there were no wide windows at the side. *Were* there any windows at all? Jack couldn't see any. Well, whatever *was* this curious van?

And where was it going? The driver simply *must* have made a mistake! The boy began to climb over the gate. Then he suddenly sat still.

The car's headlights had gone out. The car itself had stopped, and so had the thing it was towing. Jack could make out the dark shapes of the car and the van behind, standing quite still. What was it all about?

Somebody spoke to somebody else in a low voice. Jack could see that one or two men had got out of the car, but he could not hear their footsteps because of the snow.

How he wished the moon was up, then he could hide behind the hedge and see what was happening! He heard a man's voice speaking more loudly.

'Nobody about, is there?'

'Only that deaf fellow,' said another voice.

'Have a look, will you?' said the first voice. 'Just in case.'

Jack slipped quickly down from the gate, as he saw a powerful torch flash out. He crouched behind the snowy hedge, scraping snow over himself. There came the soft crunch of footsteps walking over frosty snow by the hedge. The flashlight shone over the gate and the man gave an exclamation.

'Who's there? Who are you?'

Jack's heart beat so hard against him that it hurt. He was just about to get up and show himself, and say who he was, when the man at the gate began to laugh.

'My word – look here, Nibs – a whole lot of snowmen standing out here! I thought they were alive at first, watching for us! I got a scare all right.'

Another man came softly to the first and he laughed too. 'Kids' work, I suppose,' he said. 'Yes, they look real all right, in this light. There's nobody about here at this time of night, Mac. Come on – let's get down to business.'

They went back towards the car. Jack sat up, trembling. What in the world could the men be doing down here in the snowy darkness, outside an old empty house? Should he try to see what they were up to? He didn't want to in the least. He wanted to go home as quickly as he could!

He crept to the gate again. He heard strange sounds from where the men were – as if they were unbolting something – opening the van perhaps.

And then there came a sound that sent Jack helter-skelter over the gate and up the lane as fast as his legs would take him! An angry, snorting sound, and then a curious high squeal – and then a noise of a terrific struggle, with the two men panting and grunting ferociously.

Jack couldn't think for the life of him what the noise was, and he didn't care, either. All he wanted was to get home before anything happened to *him*. Something was happening to somebody, that was certain, out there in the snowy lane. It would need a very, very brave person to go and interfere – and Jack wasn't brave at all, that night!

He came to his house, panting painfully. He crept in at the garden door and locked and bolted it. He went upstairs, not even caring if the stairs creaked under his feet! He switched on the light in his bedroom. Ah – that was better. He didn't feel so scared once he had the light on.

He looked at himself in the glass. He was very pale, and his coat was covered with snow. That was through lying in the snowy ditch below the hedge. He caught sight of his badge, still pinned on to his coat. Well, anyhow, he had *that*.

I went out to find my badge – and goodness knows what else I've found, thought the boy. Gosh – I must tell the others. We must have a meeting tomorrow. This is something for the Secret Seven! Wow! What a thrill for them!

He couldn't wait to tell them the next day. He must slip out again – and go to the shed at the bottom of Peter's garden. He must leave a note there, demanding a meeting at once!

'It's important. Very, very important,' said Jack to himself, as he scribbled a note on a bit of paper. 'It really is something for the Society to solve.'

He slipped down the stairs again, and out of the garden door. He wasn't frightened any more. He ran all the way up the lane and round to Peter's house. The farmhouse stood dark and silent. Everyone was in bed; they did not stay up late at the farm.

Jack went down to the old shed. He

fumbled at the door. It was locked. His hands felt the big letters, S.S., on the door itself. He bent down and slid his note under the crack at the bottom. Peter would find it the next day.

Then home he went again to bed – but not to sleep. Who had made that noise? What was that strange high van? Who were the men? It really was enough to keep any-body awake for hours!

[5]

Exciting plans

Next morning Janet went down to the shed by herself. Peter was brushing Scamper. He was well and truly brushed every single morning, so it was no wonder his coat shone so beautifully.

'Just open the shed and give it an airing,' ordered Peter. 'We shan't be using it today. There won't be any meeting yet.'

Janet skipped down the path, humming. She took the key from its hiding-place – a little ledge beneath the roof of the shed – and slipped it into the lock. She opened the door.

The shed smelt rather stuffy. She left the door open and went to open the little window too. When she turned round she saw Jack's note on the floor.

At first she thought it was an odd piece of waste paper, and she picked it up and crumpled it, meaning to throw it away. Then she caught sight of a word on the outside of the folded paper.

'URGENT. VERY IMPORTANT INDEED.'

She was astonished. She opened the paper out and glanced down it. Her mouth fell open in amazement. She raced out of the shed at top speed, yelling for Peter.

'Peter! PETER! Where are you? Something's happened, quick!'

Her mother heard her and called to her. 'Janet, Janet, what's the matter, dear? What's happened?'

'Oh – nothing, Mummy,' called back Janet, suddenly remembering that this was Secret Society business.

'Well, why are you screeching for Peter like that?' said her mother. 'You made me jump.'

Janet flew up the stairs to where Peter was still brushing Scamper. 'Peter! Didn't you hear me calling? I tell you, something's happened!'

'What is it?' asked Peter, surprised.

'Look – I found this paper when I went to the shed this morning,' said Janet, and she gave him Jack's note. 'It's marked "Urgent. Very Important Indeed". Look what it says inside.'

Peter read out loud what Jack had written:

Peter, call a meeting of the Secret Seven at once. Very important Mystery to solve. It happened to me last night about half-past nine. Get the others together at ten if you can. I'll be there.

Jack

'What on *earth* does he mean?' said Peter, in wonder. 'Something happened to *him* last night? Well, why is it such a mystery then? I expect he's exaggerating.'

'He's not, he's not. I'm sure he's not,' cried Janet, dancing from one foot to another in her excitement. 'Jack doesn't exaggerate, you know he doesn't. Shall I go and tell the others to come at ten if they can? Peter, it's exciting. It's a mystery!'

'You wait and see what the mystery is before you get all worked up,' said Peter, who, however, was beginning to feel rather thrilled himself. 'I'll go and tell Colin and George – you can tell the girls.'

Janet sped off in one direction and Peter in another. How lovely to have to call a meeting already – and about something so exciting too.

It was about half-past nine when the two came back. Everyone had promised to come. They were all very anxious to know what Jack had got to say.

'Remember your badges,' Janet said to the two girls. 'You won't be admitted to an important meeting like this unless you know the password and have your badge.'

Everyone turned up early, eager to hear the news. Everyone remembered the password, too.

'Weekdays!' and the door was opened and shut.

'Weekdays,' and once more the door was opened and shut. Member after member passed in, wearing the badge and murmuring the password. Both Colin and George had their badges this morning. George had found his and Colin's mother had already made him one.

Jack was the last of all to arrive, which was most annoying because everyone was dying to hear what he had to say. But he came at last.

'Weekdays,' said his voice softly, outside the shed door. It opened and he went in. Everybody looked at him expectantly.

'We got your note, and warned all the

members to attend this meeting,' said Peter. 'What's up, Jack? Is it really important?'

'Well, you listen and see,' said Jack, and he sat down on the box left empty for him. 'It happened last night.'

He began to tell his story – how he had missed his badge and felt certain he had dropped it in the field where the snowmen were – how he had slipped out with his torch to find it, and what he had heard and seen from the field.

'That frightful noise – the snorting and the horrid squeal!' he said. 'It nearly made my hair stand on end. Why did those men come down that lane late at night? It doesn't lead anywhere. It stops a little further on just by a large holly hedge. And what could that thing be that they were towing behind?'

'Was it a cage, or something – or was it a closed van where somebody was being kept prisoner?' said Barbara, in a half-whisper.

'It wasn't a cage as far as I could see,' said

Jack. 'I couldn't even see any windows to it. It was more like a small removal van than anything – but whatever was inside wasn't furniture. I tell you it snorted and squealed and struggled.'

'Was it a man inside, do you think?' asked Pam, her eyes wide with interest and excitement.

'No. I don't think so. It might have been, of course,' said Jack. 'But a man doesn't snort like that. Unless he had a gag over his mouth, perhaps.'

This was a new thought and rather an alarming one. Nobody spoke for a minute.

'Well,' said Jack, at last, 'it certainly is something for the Secret Seven to look into. There's no doubt about that. It's all very mysterious – very mysterious indeed.'

'How are we going to tackle it?' said George.

They all sat and thought. 'We had better find out if we can tell anything by the tracks in the snow,' said Peter. 'We'll find out too if there are car-tracks up the drive to that old house.'

'Yes. And we could ask the old caretaker if he heard anything last night,' said Colin.

'Bags I don't do that,' said Pam at once. 'I'd hate to go and ask him questions.'

'Well, somebody's got to,' said George. 'It might be important.'

'And we might try and find out who owns the old empty house,' said Colin.

'Yes,' said Peter. 'Well, let's split up the inquiries. Pam, you go with George and see if you can find out who owns the house.'

'How do we find out?' asked Pam.

'You will have to use your common sense,' said Peter. 'I can't decide *every*thing. Janet, you and Barbara can go down the lane and examine it for car-tracks and anything else you can think of.'

'Right,' said Janet, glad that she hadn't got to question the caretaker.

'Colin, Jack and I will go into the drive of the old house and see if we can get the caretaker to tell us anything,' said Peter, feeling rather important as he made all these arrangements.

'What's Scamper to do?' asked Janet.

'He's going to come with *us*,' said Peter. 'In case the caretaker turns nasty! Old Scamper can turn nasty too, if he has to!'

'Oh, yes – that's a good idea, to take Scamper,' agreed Jack, relieved at the thought of having the dog with him. 'Well – shall we set off?'

'Yes. Meet and report here this afternoon,' said Peter. 'You've discovered a most exciting mystery, Jack, and it's up to the Secret Seven to solve it as soon as they can!'

[6]

Finding out a few things

All the Secret Seven set off at once, feeling extremely important. Scamper went with Peter, Colin and Jack, his tail well up, and he also felt very important. He was mixed up in a Mystery with the Society! No wonder he turned up his nose at every dog he met.

They left Pam and George at the corner, looking rather worried. The two looked at one another. '*How* are we going to find out who owns the house?' said Pam.

'Ask at the post office!' said George, feeling that he really had got a very bright idea. 'Surely if the house is owned by someone who has put in a caretaker, there must be letters going there.'

'Good idea!' said Pam, and they went off to the post office. They were lucky enough to see a postman emptying the letters from the letterbox outside. George nudged Pam.

'Come on. We must start somewhere. We'll ask him!'

They went up to the man. 'Excuse me,' said George. 'Could you tell us who lives at the old house down by the stream – you know, the empty house there?'

'How can anyone live in an empty house?' said the postman. 'Don't ask silly questions and waste my time! You children – you think you're so funny, don't you?'

'We didn't mean to be funny, or cheeky either,' said Pam in a hurry. 'What George means is – who owns the house? There's a caretaker there, we know. We just wondered who the house belongs to.'

'Why? Thinking of buying it?' said the postman, and laughed at his own joke. The children laughed too, wishing the man would answer their question.

'How would I know who owns the place?' he said, emptying the last of the letters into his sack. 'I never take letters there except to old Dan the caretaker, and he only gets one once in a month – his wages, maybe. Better ask at the estate agent's over there. They deal with houses, and they might know the owner – seeing as you're so anxious to find him!'

'Oh, *thank* you,' said Pam, joyfully, and the two of them hurried across to the estate agent's. 'We might have thought of this ourselves,' said Pam. 'But hold on – what shall we say if the man here asks why we want to know? You only go to an estate agent's if you want to buy or sell a house, don't you?'

They peeped in at the door. A boy of about sixteen sat at a table there, addressing some envelopes. He didn't look very frightening. Perhaps *he* would know – and wouldn't ask them why they wanted the name of the owner.

They went boldly in. The boy looked up.

'What do you want?' he said.

'We've been told to ask who owns the old house down by the stream,' said George, hoping the boy might think that some grown-up had sent him to find out. Actually it was only Peter, of course, but he didn't see why he should say so.

'I don't think the house is on the market,' said the boy, turning over the pages of a big book. 'Do your parents want to buy it, or something? I didn't know it was to be sold.'

The two children said nothing, because they didn't really know what to say. The boy went on turning over the pages.

'Ah – here we are,' he said. 'It's not for sale – it was sold to a Mr J. Holikoff some time ago. Don't know why he doesn't live in it, I'm sure!'

'Does Mr Holikoff live anywhere here?' asked Pam.

'No – his address is 64, Heycom Street, Covelty,' said the boy, reading it out. ''Course, I don't know if he lives there now. Do your people want to get in touch with him? I can find out if this is his address now, if you like – he's on the telephone at this address.'

'Oh, no, thank you,' said George hastily. 'We don't want to know anything more, as the house is – er – not for sale. Thank you very much. Good morning.'

They went out, rather red in the face, but very pleased with themselves. 'Mr Holikoff,' said Pam to George. 'It's a peculiar name, isn't it? Do you remember his address, George?'

'Yes,' said George. He took out his notebook and wrote in it: 'Mr J. Holikoff, 64, Heycom Street, Covelty. Well, we've done our part of the job! I wonder how the others are getting on.'

They were getting on quite well. Janet and Barbara were busy examining the tracks down the lane that led to the stream. They felt quite like detectives.

'See – the car with the van behind, or whatever it was, turned into the lane from the direction of Templeton; it didn't come from our village,' said Janet. 'You can see quite clearly where the wheels almost went into the ditch.'

'Yes,' said Barbara, staring at them. 'The tracks of the van wheels are narrower than the wheels of the car that towed it, Janet. And look – just here in the snow you can see *exactly* what the pattern was on the wheels of the van. Not of the car, though – they're all blurred.'

'Don't you think it would be a good idea to take a note of the pattern of the tyre?' said Janet. 'I mean – it just *might* come in useful. And we could measure the width of the tyre print too.'

'I don't see how those things can possibly matter,' said Barbara, who wanted to go down the lane and join the three boys.

'Well, I'm going to try and copy the pattern,' said Janet firmly. 'I'd like to have *some*thing to show the boys!'

So, very carefully, she drew the pattern in her notebook. It was a funny pattern, with lines and circles and V-shaped marks. It didn't really look very good when she had done it. She had measured the print as best she could. She had no tape-measure with her, so she had placed a sheet from her notebook over the track, and had marked on it the exact size. She felt rather pleased with herself, but she did wish she had drawn the pattern better. Barbara laughed when she saw it. 'Goodness! What a mess!' she said.

Janet looked cross and shut her notebook

up. 'Let's follow the tracks down the lane now,' she said. 'We'll see exactly where they go. Not many vans come down here – we ought to be able to follow the tracks easily.'

She was quite right. It was very easy to follow them. They went on and on down the lane – and then stopped outside the old house. There were such a lot of different marks there that it was difficult to see exactly what they were – footprints, tyre-marks, places where the snow had been kicked and ruffled up – it was hard to tell anything except that this was where people had got out and perhaps had had some kind of struggle.

'Look – the tyre-marks leave all this mess and go on down the lane,' said Janet. She looked over the gate. Were the boys in the old house with the caretaker?

'Let's go and see if we can find the boys,' said Barbara.

'No. We haven't quite finished our job

yet,' said Janet. 'We ought to follow the tracks as far as they go. Come on – we'll see if they go as far as the stream. There are *two* lots of tracks all down the lane, as we saw – so it's clear that the car and trailer went down, and then up again. We'll find out where they turned.'

That was easy. The tracks went down to a field gate, almost to the stream. Someone had opened the gate, and the car had gone in with the trailer, and had made a circle there, come out of the gate again, and returned up the lane. It was all written clearly in the tyre-tracks.

'Well, that's the story of last night,' said Janet, pleased at their discoveries. 'The car and the thing it was pulling came from the direction of Templeton, turned down into this lane, stopped outside the old house, where people got out and messed around – and then went down to the field, someone opened the gate, the car and trailer went in and turned, and came out again and went up the lane – and disappeared into the night. Who or what it brought in the trailer-van goodness knows!'

'Funny thing to do at that time of night,' said Barbara.

'Very odd,' agreed Janet. 'Now let's go back to the old house and wait for the boys.'

'It's almost one o'clock,' said Barbara. 'Do you think they're still there?'

They hung over the gate and watched and listened. To their horror the old caretaker came rushing out as soon as he saw them, his big stick in his hand.

'More of you!' he cried. 'You wait till I get you. You'll feel my stick all right. Pestering, interfering children! You just wait!'

But Barbara and Janet didn't wait! They fled up the lane in fright, as fast as they could possibly go in the soft thick snow.

[7]

A talk with the caretaker

The three boys and Scamper had had an exciting time. They had gone down the lane, noting the car-tracks as they passed. They came to the old house. They saw that the gate was shut. They leaned over the top and saw tracks going up the drive.

'There's my footprints that I made yesterday morning,' said Peter, pointing to them. 'And look, you can see Scamper's paw-marks here and there too – but our tracks are all overlaid with others – bigger foot-marks – and other marks too, look – rather strange.'

'A bit like prints that would be made by someone wearing great flat, roundish slippers,' said Jack, puzzled. 'Who would wear slippers like that? Look, you can see them again and again, all over the place. Whoever wore them was prancing about a bit! Probably being dragged in.'

The boys leaned over the gate and considered all the marks carefully. They traced them with their eyes as far as they could see. 'Can any of you make out if the tracks go up the front door steps?' said Colin. 'I can't from here – but it rather looks to me as if the snow is smooth up the steps – not trampled at all.'

'I can't make out from here,' said Peter. 'Let's go up the drive. After all, we've got to interview the caretaker and find out if he heard anything last night. So we've got to go in.'

'What shall we say if he asks us why we want to know?' said Colin. 'I mean – if he's in this mystery, whatever it is, he may be frightfully angry if he thinks we know anything about it.'

'Yes, he might,' said Peter. 'We'll have to be rather clever over this. Let's think.'

They thought. 'I can't think of anything except to sort of lead him on a bit – ask him if he isn't afraid of burglars and things like that,' said Peter at last. 'See if we can make him talk.'

'All right,' said Colin. 'But it seems a bit feeble. Let's go in.'

Scamper ran ahead down the drive. He disappeared round a corner. The boys followed the footprints carefully, noting how the slipper-like ones appeared everywhere, as if the owner had gone from side to side and hopped about like mad!

'They *don't* go up the front door steps,' said Colin. 'I thought they didn't! They go round the side of the house – look here – right past the side door where the caretaker came out yesterday – and down this path – and round to the kitchen door!'

'Well – how strange!' said Peter, puzzled.

'Why did everyone go prancing round to the kitchen door when there's a front door and a side door? Yes – all three tracks are here – two sets of shoe-prints – and those funny round slipper-prints too. It beats me!'

They tried the kitchen door, but it was locked. They peered in at the window. The kitchen was completely bare and empty. But they saw a gas-stove, a sink piled with plates, and a bucket nearby when they looked through the scullery window.

'I suppose the caretaker has the use of the scullery and that front room in the house,' said Jack.

'Look out – here he is!' said Peter suddenly.

The old man was shuffling into the empty kitchen. He saw the three boys through the window and went to fling it open in a rage.

'If you want that dog of yours, he's round in the front garden!' he shouted. 'You clear out. I won't have kids round here. You'll be breaking windows before I know where I am!'

'No, we shan't,' shouted Jack, determined to make the deaf old man hear. 'We'll just collect our dog and go. Sorry he came in here.'

'Aren't you rather lonely here?' shouted Colin. 'Aren't you afraid of burglars?'

'No. I'm not afraid, ' said the old fellow, scornfully. 'I've got my big stick – and there's nothing to steal here.'

'Somebody's been round to the back door, all the same,' shouted Peter, seeing a chance to discuss this bit of mystery with the caretaker and see if he knew anything about it. He pointed to all the tracks leading to the back door. The old man leaned out of the window and looked at them.

'They're no more than the tracks you've made yourself, tramping about where you've no business to be!' he said angrily.

'They're not. I bet it was burglars or

something last night,' said Peter, and all three boys looked closely at the caretaker to see if his face changed in any way.

'Pah!' he said. 'Trying to frighten me, are you, with your silly boys' nonsense!'

'No. I'm not,' said Peter. 'Didn't you hear anything at all last night? If burglars *were* trying to get in, wouldn't you hear them?'

'I'm deaf,' said the old man. 'I wouldn't hear nothing at all – but wait now – yes, I did think I heard something last night. I'd forgotten it. Ah – that's odd, that is.'

The boys almost forgot to breathe in their excitement. 'What did you hear?' said Jack, forgetting to shout. The old man took no notice. He frowned, and his wrinkled face became even more wrinkled.

'Seems like I heard some squealing or some such noise,' he said slowly. 'I thought it was maybe some noise in my ears – I get noises often, you know – and I didn't go to see if anything was up. But, there now, nobody took nothing nor did any damage – so what's the use of bothering? If people want to squeal, let 'em, I say!'

'Was the squealing in the house?' shouted Peter.

'Well, I guess I wouldn't hear any squealing *outside*,' said the old man. 'I'm deaf as a post, usually. Ah, you're just making fun of me, you are – trying to frighten an old man. You ought to be ashamed of yourselves!'

'Can we come in and look round?' shouted Colin, and the others looked eagerly at the caretaker. If only he would say yes! But he didn't, of course.

'What are you thinking of, asking to come in!' he cried. 'I know you kids – pestering creatures – wasting my time like this. You clear out and don't you come here again with your tale of burglars and such. You keep away. Kids like you are always up to mischief.'

Just at that moment Scamper came

bounding up. He saw the old caretaker at the window and leapt up at him, in a friendly manner. The man jumped in alarm. He thought Scamper was trying to snap at him. He leaned forward and aimed a blow at him through the window with his stick. Scamper dodged and barked.

'I'm going to teach that dog a lesson!' cried the old man, in a fury. 'Yes, and you too – standing out there being cheeky! I'll teach you to make fun of me, you and your dog!'

He disappeared. 'He's going to dart out of the side door,' said Peter. 'Come on – we've learnt all we want to know. We'll go!'

[8]

Another meeting

The meeting that afternoon was very interesting and full of excitement. Everyone had something to report. They came punctually to the old shed, giving the password without a pause.

'Weekdays!'

'Weekdays!'

'Weekdays!'

One after another the Seven passed in, and soon they were sitting round the shed. They all looked very important. Scamper sat by Peter and Janet, his long ears drooping down like a judge's wig, making him look very wise.

'Pam and George – you report first,' said Peter.

So they reported, telling how they had found out that the old house had been sold to a Mr J. Holikoff some time back, although he had never lived in it.

'Did you get his address?' asked Peter. 'It might be important.'

'Yes,' said George, and produced his notebook. He read the address.

'Good. We might have to get in touch with him if we find that he ought to know something strange is going on in his empty house,' said Peter.

Pam and George felt very proud of themselves. Then the two girls reported. They told how they had discovered that the tracks came from the direction of the town of Templeton, and had gone down to the gates of the old house, where it was plain that they had stopped, as Jack had noticed the night before, when he heard the car. Then they told how the tracks had gone into the field, circled round and come out again

– and had clearly gone up the lane and back the way they came.

'Good work,' said Peter. Janet took out her notebook and went rather red in the face.

'I've just got this to report, too,' she said, showing the page of the notebook on which she had tried to draw the tyre pattern. 'I don't expect it's much use, really – it's the pattern on the tyres of the van or trailer or lorry, or whatever it was that was pulled behind the car. And I measured the width, too.'

Everyone looked at the scribbled pattern. It didn't look anything much, but Peter seemed pleased.

'Even if it's no use, it was a good idea to do it,' he said. 'Just suppose it *was* some use – and the snow melted – your drawing would be the only pattern we had to track down the tyres.'

'Yes,' said Colin, warmly. 'I think that was good, Janet.'

Janet glowed with pride. She put away her notebook. 'Now you three boys report,' she said, though she herself had already heard part of it from Peter while they were waiting for the others to come that afternoon.

Peter made the report for the three of them. Everyone listened in silence, looking very thrilled.

'So, you see,' finished Peter, '*some*body went to the old house last night, got in through the kitchen door, because the footsteps went right to there – and I think they left a prisoner behind!'

Pam gasped. 'A prisoner! What do you mean?'

'Well, isn't it clear that there was a prisoner in that big windowless van – a prisoner who was not to be seen or heard – someone who was dragged round to the kitchen and forced inside – and hidden somewhere in that house? Somebody who was hurt and who squealed loudly enough for even the old deaf caretaker to hear?' said Peter.

Everyone looked upset and uncomfortable.

'I don't like it,' said Colin. Nobody liked it. It was horrid to think of a poor, squealing prisoner locked up somewhere in that old, empty house.

'What about his food?' said Colin, at last.

'Yes – and water to drink,' said Janet. 'And *why* is he locked up there?'

'Kidnapped, perhaps,' said Jack. 'You know – this is really very serious, if we're right.'

There was a silence. 'Ought we to tell our parents?' asked Pam.

'Or the police?' said Jack.

'Well – not till we know a little bit more,' said Peter. 'There might be some quite simple explanation of all this – a car losing its way or something.'

'I've just thought of something!' said

Jack. 'That van – could it have been some sort of ambulance, do you think! You know, the van that ill people are taken to hospitals in? Maybe it was, and the car took the wrong turning, and stopped when it found it had gone wrong. And the ill person cried out with pain, or something.'

'But the caretaker said he heard squealing too, inside the house,' said Peter. 'Still, that might have been some noises in his head, of course, like those he says he sometimes has. Well – it's an idea, Jack – it *might* have been an ambulance, pulled by a car, though I can't say I've ever seen one like the one you describe.'

'Anyway, we'd better not tell anyone till we've *proved* there's something odd going on,' said Colin. 'We should feel so silly if we reported all this to the police and then they found it was just something perfectly ordinary!'

'Right. We'll keep the whole thing secret,' said Peter. 'But, of course, we've got to do something about it ourselves. We can't leave it.'

'Of *course* we've got to do something,' said George. 'But what?'

'We'll think,' said Peter. So they all thought again. What would be the best move to make next?

'I've thought of something,' said Jack at last. 'It's a bit frightening, though.'

'Whatever is it?' chorused the others.

'Well – it seems to me that if there *is* a prisoner locked up in one of the rooms of the old house, he will have to be fed and given water,' said Jack. 'And whoever does that would have to visit him at night. See? So what about us taking it in turn at night to go and watch outside the old house to see who goes in – then we might even follow them and see where they go, and who they've got there!'

'It seems a very good idea,' said Peter. 'But we'd have to watch two at a time. I wouldn't want to go and hide somewhere there all by myself!'

'*I* think that probably someone will be along tonight,' said George. 'Why shouldn't all four of us boys go and wait in hiding?'

'It would be difficult for four of us to hide and not be seen,' said Colin.

'Well – let's drape ourselves in white sheets or something and go and join the snowmen in the field!' said Peter, jokingly. To his surprise the other three boys pounced on his idea eagerly.

'Oh, *yes*, Peter – that's brilliant! Nobody would ever guess we weren't snowmen if we had something white round us!' said Colin.

'We get a good view of the lane, and could see and hear anyone coming along,' said George.

'Two could follow anyone into the house

and two remain on guard outside, as snowmen, to give warning in case the other two got into trouble,' said Jack. 'I'd love to stand there with the snowmen! We'd have to wrap up jolly warmly, though.'

'Can't we girls come too?' asked Pam.

'I don't want to!' said Barbara.

'No,' said Peter. 'I am sorry but seven is too many. We'll have more chance of success if there are only four of us.'

'What about Scamper?' asked Jack, his eyes gleaming with excitement. 'Shall we take him?'

'We'd better, I think,' said Peter. 'He'll be absolutely quiet if I tell him.'

'I'll make him a little white coat,' said Janet. 'Then he won't be seen either. He'll look like a big lump of snow or something!'

They all began to feel very excited. 'What time shall we go?' said Colin.

'Well, it was about half-past nine, wasn't it, when the men arrived last night,' said Jack. 'We'll make it the same time then. Meet here at about nine tonight. My goodness – this *is* a bit of excitement, isn't it?'

[9]

Out into the night

Janet spent the whole of the afternoon making Scamper a white coat. Peter borrowed a ragged old sheet, and found an old white macintosh. He thought he could cut up the sheet and make it do for the other three, it was so big.

Janet helped him to cut it up and make arm-holes and neck-holes. She giggled when he put one on to see if it was all right.

'You do look peculiar,' she said. 'What about your head – how are you going to hide your dark hair? It will be moonlight tonight, you know.'

'We'll have to try and make white caps or something,' said Peter. 'And we'll paint our faces white!'

'There's some whitewash in the shed,' said Janet, with another giggle. 'Oh, dear – you *will* all look strange. Can I come to the shed at nine, Peter, and just see you all before you go?'

'All right – if you can creep down without anyone seeing you,' said Peter. 'I think Mummy's going out tonight, so it should be all right. If she's not, you mustn't come in case you make a noise and spoil the whole thing.'

Mummy *was* going out that night. Good! Now it would be easy to slip down to the shed. Peter told Janet she must wrap up very warmly indeed – and if she had fallen asleep she was not to wake up!

'I *shan't* fall asleep,' said Janet, indignantly. 'You know I couldn't possibly. Mind *you* don't.'

'Don't be silly,' said Peter. 'As if the leader in an important plan like this could fall asleep! My word, Janet – the Secret Seven are in for an adventure this time!'

At half-past eight the children's lights were out, and didn't go on again. But torches lit up their rooms, and Janet was very, very busy dressing up Scamper in his new white coat. He didn't like it at all, and kept biting at it.

'Oh, Scamper – you won't be allowed to go unless you look like a snow-dog!' said Janet, almost in despair. And whether or not Scamper understood what she said she didn't know – but from that moment he let her dress him up without any more trouble. He looked peculiar and very mournful.

'Come on, if you're coming – it's almost nine,' said a whispering voice. It was Peter's. Together the two children and Scamper crept down the stairs. They were very warmly wrapped up indeed – but as soon as they got out into the air they found that it was not nearly as cold as they expected.

'The snow's melting! There's no frost tonight,' whispered Janet.

'Gosh, I hope those snowmen won't have melted,' said Peter, in alarm.

'Oh, they won't *yet*,' said Janet. 'Come on – I can see one of the others.'

The passwords were whispered softly at the door of the shed, and soon there were five of the Secret Seven there. Peter lit a candle, and they all looked at one another in excitement.

'We've got to paint our faces white and put on our white things,' said Peter. 'Then we're ready.'

Jack giggled. 'Look at Scamper! He's in white too! Scamper, you look ridiculous.'

'Woof,' said Scamper, miserably. He *felt* ridiculous, too! Poor Scamper.

With squeals and gurgles of laughter the four boys painted their faces white. They had carefully put on their white things first so as not to mess up their overcoats. Janet fitted the little white skull caps she had roughly made, over each boy's head.

'Well! I shouldn't like to meet you walking down the lane tonight!' she said. 'You look terrifying!'

'Time we went,' said Peter. 'Goodbye, Janet. Go to bed now and sleep tight. I'll tell you our adventures in the morning! I shan't wake you when I come in.'

'I shall stay awake till you come!' said Janet.

She watched them go off down the moonlit path, a row of weird white figures with horrid white faces. They really did look like walking snowmen, as they trod softly over the soft, melting snow.

They made their way quietly out of the gate and walked in the direction of the lane that led to the old house, keeping a sharp lookout for any passers-by.

They met no one except a big boy who came so quietly round a corner in the snow that not one of the four heard him. They stopped at once when they saw him.

He stopped too. He gazed at the four white snowmen in horror.

'Ooooh!' he said. 'Ow! What's this? Who are you?'

Peter gave a dreadful groan, and the boy yelled in alarm. 'Help! Four live snowmen! Help!'

He tore off down the road, shouting. The four boys collapsed in helpless giggles against the fence behind.

'Oh, dear!' said Jack. 'I nearly burst with laughter when you did that groan, Peter.'

'Come on – we'd better get away quickly before the boy brings somebody back here,' and they went chuckling on their way. They came to the lane where the old house stood and went down it. They soon came to the old house. It stood silent and dark, with its roof white in the moonlight.

'Nobody's here yet,' said Peter. 'There's no light anywhere in the house, and not a sound to be heard.'

'Let's go and join the merry gang of snowmen then,' said Jack. 'And I wish you'd tell Scamper not to get between my feet so much, Peter. He'll trip me up in this sheet thing I'm wearing.'

They climbed over the gate and went into the field. The snowmen still stood there, but alas! they were melting and were already smaller than they had been in the morning. Scamper went and sniffed at each one solemnly. Peter called him.

'Come here! You've got to stand as still as we do – and remember, not a bark, not a growl, not a whine!'

Scamper understood. He stood as still as a statue beside Peter. The boys looked for all the world like neat snowmen as they stood there in the snowy field.

They waited and they waited. Nobody came. They waited for half an hour and then they began to feel cold. 'The snow is melting round my feet,' complained Jack.

'How much longer do you think we've got to stand here?'

The others felt tired of it too. Gone were their ideas of staying half the night standing quietly with the snowmen! Half an hour was more than enough.

'Can't we go for a little walk, or something?' said Colin, impatiently. 'Just to get us warm.'

Peter was about to answer when he stopped and stiffened. He had heard something. What was it?

Colin began to speak again. 'Sh!' said Peter. Colin stopped at once. They all listened. A faraway sound came to their straining ears.

'It's that squealing noise,' said Jack, suddenly. 'I know it is! Only very faint and far away. It's coming from the old house. There is somebody there!'

Shivers went down their backs. They listened again, and once more the strange, faraway sound came on the night air.

'I don't like it,' said Peter. 'I'm going to the old house to see if I can hear it there. I think we ought to tell someone.'

'Let's all go,' said Colin. But Peter was quite firm about that.

'No. Two to go and two to remain on guard. That's what we said. Jack, you come with me. Colin and George, stay here and watch.'

Peter and Jack, two weird white figures with strange white faces, went to the field gate, climbed it, and went to the gate of the old house. They opened it and shut it behind them. There was no noise at all to be heard now.

They went quietly up the drive, keeping to the shadows in case the old caretaker might possibly be looking out. They went to the front door and looked through the letterbox. Nothing was to be seen through there at all. All was dark inside.

They went to the side door. It was fastened, of course. Then they went to the back door and tried that. That was locked, too. Then they heard a strange thudding, thundering noise from somewhere in the house. They clutched at one another. What *was* going on in this old empty house?

'Look! That old man has left this window a bit open – the one he spoke to us out of this morning,' whispered Jack, suddenly.

'Goodness – has he, really? Then what about getting in and seeing if we can find the prisoner?' whispered Peter, in excitement.

It only took a minute or two to climb up and get inside. They stood in the dark kitchen, listening. There was no noise to be heard at all. Where could the prisoner be?

'Dare we search the whole house from top to bottom?' said Peter. 'I've got my torch.'

'Yes, we dare, because we must,' answered Jack. So, as quietly as they could they tiptoed into first the scullery and then an outhouse. Nobody there at all.

'Now into the hall and we'll peep into the rooms there,' said Peter.

The front rooms were bright with moonlight but the back rooms were dark. The boys pushed open each door and flashed the torch round the room beyond. Each one was silent and empty.

They came to a shut door. Sounds came from behind it. Peter clutched Jack. 'Somebody's in here. I expect the door's locked, but I'll try it. Stand ready to run if we're chased!'

[10]

In the old empty house

The door wasn't locked. It opened quietly. The sounds became loud at once. Somebody was in there, snoring!

The same thought came to both boys at once. It must be the caretaker! Quietly Peter looked in.

Moonlight filled the room. On a low, untidy bed lay the old caretaker, not even undressed! He looked dirty and shabby, and he was snoring as he slept. Peter turned to go – and his torch suddenly knocked against the door and fell with a crash to the floor.

He stood petrified, but the old man didn't stir. Then Peter remembered how deaf he was! Thank goodness – he hadn't even *heard* the noise! He shut the door quietly and the two boys stood out in the hall. Peter tried his torch to see if he had broken it. No, it was all right. Good.

'Now we'll go upstairs,' he whispered. 'You're not afraid, are you, Jack?'

'Not very,' said Jack. 'Just a *bit*. Come on.'

They went up the stairs that creaked and cracked in a very tiresome manner. Up to the first floor with five or six rooms to peep into – all as empty as one another. Then up to the top floor.

'We'll have to be careful now,' said Jack. He spoke in such a whisper that Peter could hardly hear him. 'These are the only rooms we haven't been into. The prisoner must be here somewhere.'

All the doors were ajar! Well, then, how could there be a prisoner – unless he was tied up? The two boys looked into each room, half-scared in case they saw something horrid.

But there was absolutely nothing there at all. The rooms were either dark and empty, or full of moonlight and nothing else.

'It's strange, isn't it?' whispered Jack. 'Honestly I don't understand it. Surely those noises *did* come from the house somewhere? Yet there's nothing and no one here except the old caretaker!'

They stood there, wondered what to do next – and once more that faraway, muffled squealing came on the night air, a kind of whinnying noise, followed by a series of curious thuds and crashes.

'There *is* a prisoner here somewhere – and he's knocking for help – and squealing too,' said Peter, forgetting to whisper. 'Somewhere downstairs. But we've looked everywhere.'

Jack was making for the stairs. 'Come on – we must have missed a cupboard or something!' he called.

Down they went, not caring now about

the noise they made. They came to the kitchen. The noises had stopped again. Then the thudding began once more. Jack clutched Peter.

'I know where it's coming from – under our feet! There's a cellar there. *That's* where the prisoner is!'

'Look for the cellar door then,' said Peter. They found it at last, in a dark corner of the passage between kitchen and scullery. They turned the handle – and what a surprise – the door opened!

'It's not locked!' whispered Jack. 'Why doesn't the prisoner escape then?'

Stone steps led downwards into the darkness. Peter flashed his torch down them. He called, in rather a shaky voice:

'Who's there? Who is it down there?'

There was no answer at all. The boys listened with straining ears. They could distinctly hear the sound of very heavy breathing, loud and harsh.

'We can hear you breathing!' called Jack. 'Do tell us who you are. We've come to rescue you.'

Still no reply. This was dreadful. Both boys were really scared. They didn't dare to go down the steps. Their legs simply refused to move downwards. Yet it seemed very cowardly to go back into the passage again.

And then another sound came to them – the sound of low voices somewhere! Then came the sound of a key being turned in a lock – and a door being opened!

Jack clutched Peter in a panic. 'It's those men I heard last night. They're back again. Quick – we must hide before they find us here.'

The two boys, strange little figures in white, stood for a moment, not knowing where to go. Then Peter stripped off his white covering and cap. 'Take yours off, too,' he whispered to Jack. 'We shan't be so easily seen in our dark coats, if we slip into the shadows somewhere.'

They threw their things into a corner and then slipped into the hall. They crouched there in a corner, hoping that the men would go straight down into the cellar.

But they didn't. 'Better see if that old caretaker is asleep,' said a voice, and two men came into the hall to open the caretaker's door.

And then one of them caught sight of Peter's whitewashed face, which gleamed eerily out of the middle of the dark shadows. Peter had forgotten his face was white!

'Good gracious – look there – in that corner! Whatever is it?' cried one of the men. 'Look – over there, Mac.'

The men looked towards the corner where the two boys were crouching. 'Faces! White faces!' said the other man. 'I don't like it. Here, switch on your torch. It's just a trick of the moonlight or something.'

A powerful torch was switched on, and the two boys were discovered at once! With a few strides the man called Mac went over to them. He picked up both boys at once, gave them a rough shake and set them on their feet.

'Now then – what's the meaning of this – hiding here with your faces all painted up like that! What are you doing?'

'Let go of my arm. You're hurting,' said Jack, angrily. 'The thing is – what are *you* up to?'

'What do you mean?' said the man roughly.

The thudding noise began again, and the two boys looked at the men.

'That's what I mean,' said Jack. 'Who's down there? Who are you keeping prisoner?'

Jack got a clout on the head that made him see stars. Then he and Peter were dragged to a nearby cupboard and locked in. The men seemed furiously angry for some reason or other.

Peter put his ear to the crack and tried to hear what they were saying.

'What are we going to do now? If those kids get anyone here, we're done.'

'Right. Keep the kids here too, then. Put them down with Kerry Blue! We'll fetch him tomorrow night and clear off, and nobody will know anything. The job will be done by then.'

'What about the kids?'

'We'll leave them locked up here – and send a card to the old caretaker to tell him to look down in his cellar the day after tomorrow. He'll get a shock when he finds the kids prisoners there! Serve them right, little pests.'

Peter listened. Who was Kerry Blue? What a peculiar name! He trembled when he heard the men coming to the door. But they didn't unlock it. One of them called through the crack.

'You can stay there for a while. Teach

you to come poking your noses into what's no business of yours!'

Then began various curious noises. Something seemed to be brought into the scullery. The boys heard the crackling of wood as if a fire was being lit. Then a nasty smell came drifting through the cracks of the door.

'Oooh! They're boiling something. Whatever is it?' said Peter. 'Horrible smell!'

They couldn't think what it was. They heard a lot of squealing again, and some snorting, and a thundering noise like muffled hooves thudding on stone. It was all very, very extraordinary.

The cupboard, made to take a few coats, was small and cold and airless. The two boys were very uncomfortable. They were glad when one of the men unlocked the door and told them to come out.

'Now, you let us go,' began Peter, and got a rough blow on his shoulder at once.

'No cheek from you,' said one of the men and hustled the boys to the cellar door. He thrust both of them through it, and they half-fell down the top steps. The door shut behind them. They could hear it being locked. Blow, bother! Bother! Now *they* were prisoners too!

A noise came from below them. Oh dear – was Kerry Blue down there, whoever he was? 'Switch your torch on,' whispered Jack. 'For goodness' sake let's have a look at the prisoner and see what he's like!'

[11]

The prisoner

Peter switched on his torch, his hand trembling as he did so. What were they going to see?

What they saw was so surprising that both boys gave a gasp of amazement. They were looking down on a beautiful horse, whose pricked ears and rolling eyes showed that he was as scared as they were!

'A *horse*!' said Jack, feebly. 'It's a *horse*!'

'Yes – that squealing was its frightened whinny – and thudding was its hooves on the stone floor when it rushed about in panic,' said Peter. 'Oh, Jack – poor, poor thing! How *wicked* to keep a horse down here like this! Why do they do it!'

'It's such a beauty. It looks like a racehorse,' said Jack. 'Do you suppose they've stolen it? Do you think they're hiding it here till they can change it to another colour, or something – horse thieves do do that, you know – and then sell it somewhere under a different name?'

'I don't know. You may be right,' said Peter. 'I'm going down to him.'

'Aren't you afraid?' said Jack. 'Look at his rolling eyes!'

'No, I'm not afraid,' said Peter, who was quite used to the horses on his father's farm, and had been brought up with them since he was a baby. 'Poor thing – it wants talking to and calming.'

Peter went down the steps, talking as he went. 'So you're Kerry Blue, are you? And a beautiful name it is, too, for a beautiful horse! Don't be frightened, beauty. I'm your friend. Just let me stroke that velvety nose of yours and you'll be all right!'

The horse squealed and shied away. Peter

took no notice. He went right up to the frightened creature and rubbed his hand fearlessly down its soft nose. The horse stood absolutely still. Then it suddenly nuzzled against the boy and made funny little snorting sounds.

'Jack, come on. The horse is friendly now,' called Peter. 'He's such a beauty. What brutes those men are to keep a horse down in a dark cellar like this. It's enough to make it go mad!'

Jack came down the steps. He stroked the horse's back and then gave an exclamation. 'Ugh! He feels sticky and wet!'

Peter shone his torch on to the horse's coat. It gleamed wetly. 'Jack! You were right! Those men *have* been dyeing him!' cried Peter. 'His coat's still wet with the dye.'

'And that's the horrid smell we smelt – the dye being boiled up ready to use,' said Jack. 'Poor old Kerry Blue! What have they been doing to you?'

The horse had a mass of straw in one corner and a rough manger of hay in another. Oats were in a heavy pail. Water was in another pail.

'Well, if *we* want a bed, we'll have to use the straw,' said Peter. 'And have oats for a feed!'

'We shan't need to,' said Jack. 'I bet old Colin and George will come and look for us soon. We'll shout the place down as soon as we hear them!'

They settled down on the straw to wait. Kerry Blue decided to lie down on the straw too. The boys leaned against his warm body, wishing he didn't smell so strongly of dye.

Up in the field, where the snow was now rapidly melting, Colin and George had been waiting impatiently for a long time. They had seen Jack and Peter disappear over the gate, and had had a difficult time holding Scamper back, because he wanted to follow them. They had stood there quietly for about half an hour, wondering whenever Peter and Jack were coming back, when Scamper began to growl.

'He can hear something,' said Colin. 'Yes – a car – coming down the lane. I do hope it's not those men again. Jack and Peter will be caught, if so!'

The car had no trailer-van behind it this time. It stopped at the gate of the old house and two men got out. Scamper suddenly barked loudly, and was at once cuffed by Colin. 'Idiot!' hissed Colin. 'Now you've given us away!'

One of the men came to the field gate at once. He gazed at the six snowmen. 'Come and look here!' he called to the other man, who went to stand beside him. How Colin and George trembled and quaked!

'What? Oh, we saw the snowmen there last night. Don't you remember?' he said. 'Some kids have been messing about again today and built a few more. Come on. That dog we heard barking must be a stray one about somewhere.'

The men left the gate and went up the drive to the house. Colin and George breathed freely again. That was a narrow escape! Thank goodness for their white faces, caps and sheets! Thank goodness Scamper was in white, too.

For a long time there was no sound at all. Colin and George got colder and colder and more and more impatient. WHAT was happening? They wished they knew. Were Jack and Peter caught?

At last, just as they thought they really must give up and go and scout round the house themselves to see what was happening, they heard sounds again. Voices! Ah, the men were back again. There was the sound of a car door being shut quietly. The engine started up. The car moved down the lane to turn in at the field gate again, go round in a circle and come out facing up the lane. It went by quickly, squelching in the soft, melting snow.

'They're gone,' said Colin. 'And we were real idiots not to have stolen up to the gate and taken the car's number! Now it's too late.'

'Yes. We *could* have done that,' said George. 'What shall we do now? Wait to see if Peter and Jack come out?'

'Yes, but not for too long,' said Colin. 'My feet are really frozen.'

They waited for about five minutes, and still no Peter or Jack came. So, sloshing through the fast-melting snow, the two boys went to the gate. They climbed over. Soon they were in the drive of the old house, hurrying up to the front door, with Scamper at their heels.

But, of course, they couldn't get in there, nor in the other doors either. And then, like Jack and Peter, they discovered the open window! In they went. They stood on the kitchen floor and listened. They could hear nothing at all.

They called softly. 'Jack! Peter! Are you here?'

Nobody answered. Not a sound was to be heard in the house. Then Scamper gave a loud bark and ran into the passage between the scullery and the kitchen. He scraped madly at a door there.

The boys followed at once, and no sooner had they got there than they heard Peter's voice.

'Who's there? That you, Colin and George? Say the password if it's you!'

'Weekdays! Where are you?' called George.

'Down here, in the cellar. We'll come up,' said Peter's voice. 'We're all right. Can you unlock the door – or has the key been taken?'

'No, it's here,' said Colin. 'Left in the door.'

He turned the key and unlocked the door. He pushed it open just as Jack and Peter came up to the top of the cellar steps!

And behind them came somebody else – somebody whose feet made a thudding sound on the stone steps – Kerry Blue! He wasn't going to be left behind in the dark cellar, all alone! He was going to stay with these nice kind boys.

Colin and George gaped in astonishment. They stared at Kerry Blue as if they had never seen a horse in their lives before. A horse – down in the cellar – locked up with Peter and Jack. How extraordinary!

'Have the men gone?' asked Peter, and Colin nodded.

'Yes. Away in their car. That's why we came to look for you. They saw us in the field because Scamper barked – but they thought we were just snowmen! What happened here?'

'Let's get out of the house,' said Peter. 'I just can't bear being here any longer.'

He led Kerry Blue behind him, and Colin was surprised that the horse made so little noise on the wooden floor of the kitchen. He looked down at the horse's hooves and gave an exclamation.

'Look! What's he's got on his feet?'

'Felt slippers, made to fit his great hooves,' said Peter, with a grin. 'That explains the curious prints we saw in the snow. I guess he had those on so that he wouldn't make too much noise down in the cellar! My word, he *was* scared when we found him. Come on – I'm going home!'

[12]

The end of the adventure

Six figures went up the snowy lane – two boys in dark anoraks, two in curious white garments and caps, a dog in a draggled white coat, and a proud and beautiful horse. All the boys had gleaming white faces and looked extremely weird, but as they didn't meet anyone it didn't matter.

Peter talked hard as he went, telling of all that had happened to him and Jack. Colin and George listened in astonishment, half-jealous that they, too, had not shared in the whole of the night's adventure.

'I'm going to put Kerry Blue into one of the stables at our farmhouse,' said Peter. 'He'll be all right now. What a shock for the men to find him gone! And tomorrow we'll tell the police. Meet at half-past nine – and collect Pam and Barbara on the way, will you? This really has been a wonderful mystery, and I do think the Secret Seven have done well! Goodness, I'm tired. I shall be asleep as soon as my head hits the pillow!'

They were all in bed and asleep in under half an hour. Janet was fast asleep when Peter got in. He had carefully stabled Kerry Blue who was now quite docile and friendly.

In the morning, what an excitement! Peter told his father and mother what had happened and his father, in amazement, went to examine Kerry Blue.

'He's a very fine racehorse,' he said. 'And he's been dyed with some kind of brown stuff, as you can see. I expect those fellows meant to sell him and race him under another name. Well, you've stopped that, you and your Society, Peter!'

'What about getting on to the police

now?' said the children's mother, anxiously. 'It does seem to me they ought to be after these men at once.'

'There's a meeting of the Secret Seven down in the shed at half-past nine,' said Peter. 'Perhaps the police could come to it.'

'Oh, no – I hardly think the police would want to sit on your flowerpots and boxes,' said Mummy. 'You must all meet in Daddy's study. That's the proper place.'

So, at half-past nine, when the Seven were all waiting in great excitement, and Scamper was going quite mad, biting a corner of the rug, the bell rang, and in walked two big policemen. They looked most astonished to see so many children sitting round in a ring.

'Good morning,' said the Inspector. 'Er – what is all this about? You didn't say much on the phone, sir.'

'No. I wanted you to hear the story from the children,' said Peter's father. He unfolded the morning paper and laid it out flat on the table. The children crowded round.

On the front page was a big photograph of a lovely horse. Underneath it were a few sentences in big black letters.

KERRY BLUE STOLEN.

FAMOUS RACEHORSE DISAPPEARS.

NO SIGN OF HIS HIDING-PLACE.

'I expect you saw that this morning,' said Peter's father. 'Peter, tell him where Kerry Blue is.'

'In our stables!' said Peter, and thoroughly enjoyed the look of utter amazement that came over the faces of the two policemen.

They got out notebooks. 'This is important, sir,' said the Inspector to Peter's father. 'Can you vouch for the fact that you've got the horse?'

'Oh, yes – there's no doubt about it,' said

Peter's father. 'You can see him whenever you like. Peter, tell your story.'

'We're going to take it in turns to tell bits,' said Peter. He began. He told about how they had made snowmen in the field. Then Jack went on to tell how he had gone to look for his Secret Seven badge in the field, and how he had seen the car and its trailer-van.

'Of course I know now it was a horse-box,' he said. 'But I didn't know then. I couldn't think what it was – it looked like a small removal van, or something. I couldn't see any proper windows either.'

So the story went on – how they had interviewed the caretaker and what he had said – how they had tracked the car down to the field gate and up the lane again. Then how four boys had dressed up as snowmen with Scamper and gone to watch.

Then came the exciting bit about Peter and Jack creeping into the house to find the prisoner – and being caught themselves. And then Colin and George took up the tale and told how they in their turn went into the old house to find Jack and Peter.

'Adventurous kids, aren't they?' said the Inspector, with a twinkle in his eye, turning to Peter's mother.

'Very,' she said. 'But I don't at all approve of this night-wandering business, Inspector. They should all have been in bed and asleep.'

'Quite,' said the Inspector. 'I agree with you. They should have told the police, no doubt about that, and left *them* to solve the mystery. Wandering about at night dressed up as snowmen – I never heard anything like it!'

He spoke in such a severe voice that the children felt quite alarmed. Then he smiled and they saw that actually he was very pleased with them.

'I'll have to find out the name of the

owner of the old house,' he said, 'and see if he knows anything about these goings-on.'

'It's a Mr Holikoff, 64, Heycom Street, Covelty,' said George at once. 'We – Pam and I – found that out.'

'Good work!' said the Inspector, and the other policeman wrote the address down at once. 'Very good work indeed.'

'I suppose they don't know the number of the car, do they?' asked the second policeman. 'That would be a help.'

'No,' said Colin, regretfully. 'But the other two girls here know something about the horse-box, sir. They took the measurements of the tyres and even drew a copy of the pattern on them – it showed in the snow, you see.'

'Janet did that,' said Barbara, honestly, wishing she hadn't laughed at Janet for doing it. Janet produced the paper on which she had drawn the pattern and taken the measurements. The Inspector took it at once, looking very pleased.

'Splendid. Couldn't be better! It's no good looking for tracks today, of course, because the snow's all melted. This is a very, very valuable bit of evidence. Dear me, what bright ideas you children have!'

Janet was scarlet with pleasure. Peter looked at her and smiled proudly. She was a fine sister to have – a really good member of the Secret Seven!

'Well, these children seem to have done most of the work for us,' said the Inspector, shutting his notebook. 'They've got the address of the owner – and if he happens to have a horse-box in his possession, whose tyres match these measurements and this pattern, then he'll have to answer some very awkward questions.'

The police went to see Kerry Blue. The children crowded into the stable too, and Kerry Blue put his ears back in alarm. But

Peter soon soothed him.

'Yes. He's been partly dyed already,' said the Inspector, feeling his coat. 'If he'd had one more coat of colour he'd be completely disguised! I suppose those fellows meant to come along and do that tonight – and then take him off to some other stable. But, of course, they had to hide him somewhere safe while they changed the colour of his coat – and so they chose the cellars of the old empty house – belonging to Mr J. Holikoff. Well, well, well – I wonder what *he* knows about it!'

The children could hardly wait to hear the end of the adventure. They heard about it at the very next meeting of the Secret Seven – which was called, not by the members themselves, but by Peter's father and mother.

It was held in the shed, and the two grown-ups had the biggest boxes as seats. Janet and Peter sat on the floor.

'Well,' said Peter's father. 'Mr Holikoff *is*

the owner of the horse-box – and of the car as well. The police waited in the old house for the two men last night – and they came! They are now safely under lock and key. They were so surprised when they found Kerry Blue gone that they hardly struggled at all!'

'Who does Kerry Blue belong to, Daddy?' said Peter. 'The papers said he was owned by Colonel James Healey. Is he sending someone to fetch him?'

'Yes,' said his father. 'He's sending off a horse-box for him today. And he has also sent something for the Secret Seven. Perhaps you'd like to see what it is, Peter.'

Peter took an envelope from his father and opened it. Out fell a shower of tickets. Janet grabbed one.

'Oooh – a circus ticket – and a pantomime ticket too! Are there seven of each?'

There were! Two lovely treats for everyone – except Scamper.

'But he can have a great big delumptious,

scrumplicious bone, can't he, Mummy?' cried Janet, hugging him.

'Whatever are you talking about? Is that some foreign language?' asked her mother in astonishment, and everyone laughed.

On the envelope was written, 'For the Secret Seven Society, with my thanks and best wishes, J. H.'

'How very kind of him,' said Peter. 'We didn't want any reward at all. The adventure was enough reward – it was brilliant!'

'Well, we'll leave you to talk about it,' said his mother, getting up. 'Or else we shall find that *we* belong to your Society too, and that it's the Secret Nine, instead of the Secret Seven!'

'No – it's the Secret *Seven*,' said Peter, firmly. 'The best Society in the world. Hurrah for the Secret Seven!'

HODDER

A complete list of the SECRET SEVEN ADVENTURES *by Enid Blyton*

1 THE SECRET SEVEN
2 SECRET SEVEN ADVENTURE
3 WELL DONE SECRET SEVEN
4 SECRET SEVEN ON THE TRAIL
5 GO AHEAD SECRET SEVEN
6 GOOD WORK SECRET SEVEN
7 SECRET SEVEN WIN THROUGH
8 THREE CHEERS SECRET SEVEN
9 SECRET SEVEN MYSTERY
10 PUZZLE FOR THE SECRET SEVEN
11 SECRET SEVEN FIREWORKS
12 GOOD OLD SECRET SEVEN
13 SHOCK FOR THE SECRET SEVEN
14 LOOK OUT SECRET SEVEN
15 FUN FOR THE SECRET SEVEN

HODDER

A complete list of the FAMOUS FIVE ADVENTURES *by Enid Blyton*

---

1 FIVE ON A TREASURE ISLAND
2 FIVE GO ADVENTURING AGAIN
3 FIVE RUN AWAY TOGETHER
4 FIVE GO TO SMUGGLER'S TOP
5 FIVE GO OFF IN A CARAVAN
6 FIVE ON KIRRIN ISLAND AGAIN
7 FIVE GO OFF TO CAMP
8 FIVE GET INTO TROUBLE
9 FIVE FALL INTO ADVENTURE
10 FIVE ON A HIKE TOGETHER
11 FIVE HAVE A WONDERFUL TIME
12 FIVE GO DOWN TO THE SEA
13 FIVE GO TO MYSTERY MOOR
14 FIVE HAVE PLENTY OF FUN
15 FIVE ON A SECRET TRAIL
16 FIVE GO TO BILLYCOCK HILL
17 FIVE GET INTO A FIX
18 FIVE ON FINNISTON FARM
19 FIVE GO TO DEMON'S ROCKS
20 FIVE HAVE A MYSTERY TO SOLVE
21 FIVE ARE TOGETHER AGAIN